Hallowed Eve, Hallowed Day

A Supernatural Suspense Story

To Jim,

Best Wishes!

Joe Rogers

Hallowed Eve, Hallowed Day
A Supernatural Suspense Story

"The issue is now quite clear. It is between light and darkness and every one must choose his side."
G.K. Chesterton

"To love is to know we are immersed not in darkness, but in light."
Mother Teresa of Calcutta

Part 1
The Night of the Boy with the Heart of Fire

While running as fast as he could, Justin Jordan looked over his shoulder at his pursuer. A strange carriage pulled by a spectral horse and driven by some sort of ghoul was about half a block behind Justin.

He didn't know why he was being pursued or what terrible fate awaited him if he was captured. The ghostly carriage was not especially swift, but it traveled faster than Justin could run and was steadily gaining on him.

On many previous nights, the ghoul driving the carriage had chased Justin through the streets of his town. Fortunately, on all those occasions, Justin had always been able to elude the ghoul. Tonight, though, the ghoul seemed relentless.

Justin had been running for several minutes and was almost completely out of breath. He knew that he could not keep running much longer. Justin desperately looked around for someplace to hide.

However, he could find no hiding place and, even if he did spot a good hiding place, he had no way to get into it unobserved. The ghoulish driver's hate-filled eyes were locked upon him liked a laser beam.

Justin rounded another corner and started to dash down that street. Then, to his dismay, he spotted new horrors up ahead. Over twenty giant spiders were scurrying down the street toward him. Each black spider was about the size of a toaster. Their white web extended from one side of the street to the other, completely blocking his passage along that road.

Justin came to a stop on the sidewalk. He could go neither forward nor backward; he had nowhere to go. An overwhelming feeling of despair paralyzed him. I wonder which one of them will kill me, Justin thought as he watched the ghoul and spiders closing in on him.

Perhaps the ghoul and the spiders will fight each other over me, and I can escape in the confusion, he thought with a slight glimmer of hope. Or perhaps someone will rescue me. Surely goodness exists somewhere in this nightmare world. I have never seen anything except horrors here, yet I feel someone else is watching and waiting.

That was when it happened.

A little blondish girl, who appeared to be about seven years old, almost casually came out the front door of a house on the street. She was bouncing a ball on a long stick, and she seemed completely intent on her game. The little girl did not appear to notice either the ghoulish carriage or the spiders.

She stepped into the street as the carriage came barreling toward her.

"Watch out!" Justin shouted to warn her.

In response, she glanced up and looked at the carriage. The little girl batted the ball away, stepped up onto the curb, and then stuck her long stick into the front wheel spokes of the carriage as it passed by.

The stick did not break, and the front wheel was unable to turn. There was a terrible screech, then a shattering sound as the carriage smashed apart, and the ghoul and his spectral horse went tumbling into the spiders' web.

Justin was glad for the reprieve, but he had not forgotten about the other grave danger.

"Look out for the spiders!" he warned the girl. "Get back into your house."

She smiled at him and shook her head. "No. It's okay. My friend will take care of the spiders."

The girl pointed across the street where a taller, brown-haired girl stood. This girl held up a lantern from which a dozen beams of light radiated. Looking intently at the spiders, she rotated the lantern so that the light beams struck them. Each spider burned away into nothingness when touched by a light beam.

The taller girl set her lantern down on the sidewalk.

"Well, I suppose that takes care of that!" she declared happily, smiling at Justin.

"Who are the two of you?" Justin asked, glancing at the girls who stood across the street from each other.

"Oh, we were sent to help you," the smaller girl replied. "You were in great danger. This dream tonight was different from the other dreams that you had in recent weeks."

"Yes," added her taller friend across the street. "They were trying to take possession of you. They wanted to claim you as one of their own. But we wouldn't allow that to happen."

Justin felt himself beginning to wake up. For the first time in a long time, he did not want to awake yet. He wanted to continue speaking with these girls.

"Are the two of you part of my dream?" he asked quickly.

The smaller girl laughed. "No. We are quite real -- as real as you are, Justin."

"You won't be bothered by any more nightmares for a while," the taller girl assured him.

Then he was awake.

Over the next three years, Justin often reflected about that dream. The taller girl had spoken truly -- there had been no more nightmares. That particular dream had ended so pleasantly that he did not think of it as a nightmare. It was a good dream.

However, in the weeks before being rescued by the two mysterious girls, Justin had suffered through many awful nightmares. Most of them involved being pursued by the evil ghoul in the carriage, but he had also been terrorized by witches and psychotic killers.

He had often awoken screaming at the top of his voice. His parents had him speak with the school counselor, then arranged for Justin to have several sessions with a private therapist. The consensus was that Justin needed to completely stop watching horror movies. He had a good memory and imagination; the horrific images of those movies were engraining themselves deep in his mind.

Justin never went to the so-called "haunted houses" at Halloween in which actors portraying demonic figures and psychotic murderers would jump out at visitors touring the house. Such scenes might cause nightmares.

He became careful about what he watched and read.
Justin tried to fill his mind with positive, life-affirming
images.

Everything went well for several more years.
However, during his sophomore year of college, an attack
came without warning.

After completing his mid-term exams, Justin had
gone out partying with some friends. He returned to his
dorm room at about 3 o'clock in the morning and
collapsed exhausted in bed.

He found himself walking down the street where the
two girls had rescued him years ago. Although nothing
threatened him at the moment, Justin was instantly on
guard because he knew that some grave danger could
appear at any moment.

He did not have long to wait. At the end of the
street, he spotted the wreckage of the ghoulish carriage.
Justin turned and began heading in the opposite direction;
he wanted to get as far away from that carriage as possible.

"Where are you going, boy?" a rasping voice called

to him. "It's been quite a while, but I haven't forgotten about you."

Justin looked back to see the ghoulish driver pushing his carriage upright. It was the first time that the ghoul had ever spoken to him. A chill ran through the length of his body.

Justin started to run toward a side street, but then he stopped, turned back, and looked at the ghoul.

"You terrorized me during my childhood, but I'm not going to allow you to do so any longer," Justin said. "I'm an adult now. I'm not afraid of you. If you want to fight, I'm ready for you."

The ghoul hesitated. "You've gotten brave, boy. Unfortunately for you, I am an immortal spirit, and you have no chance against me."

The ghoul charged at him, moving with such speed that Justin did not have time to defend himself. The ghoul struck him with a staff, sending Justin reeling onto the pavement.

The pain of the blow surprised Justin. This is a dream, he then remembered. Justin tried to wake up, but alcohol and exhaustion kept him unconscious. Within seconds, he sank deeper into the dream and, once again, forgot that he was dreaming.

The ghoul advanced on him and raised the staff, preparing to strike Justin again.

"You really are a tiresome creature," a child's lilting voice came from nearby.

As Justin forced himself to his feet, he saw the two girls who had rescued him years ago.

"Yes, when we cast you out last time, we did not expect you to return," the taller girl added.

"Meddle not where you are not wanted," the ghoul hissed at them.

"Oh, we are wanted -- just not by you," the smaller girl said.

"I'll destroy the two of you, then the boy," the ghoul said.

"Really? I think not," the smaller girl said. She glanced toward the house from which they had emerged. "Here, kitty cat!" she called.

The door flew open, and a giant black cat came bounding into the street. It was at least 9-feet high, and its eyes glowed with a yellow luminescence.

As the giant cat's eyes focused upon the ghoul, the cat coiled as it prepared to strike.

The ghoul turned and began to run back toward its carriage, but the cat sprang through the air and grabbed the ghoul in its teeth. The cat's head moved from side to side as it tore apart its enemy. Then the cat hurled the ghoul from its mouth into the air and over the carriage. In the night sky, the ghoul appeared to dissolve into nothingness.

"Once again, I can't thank you enough." He glanced up at the giant cat. "What is he?"

"Oh, that's our kitty cat," the smaller girl said. "He's very nice."

The cat looked very pleased with himself. His broad grin reminded Justin of the phrase "grinning like the Cheshire cat."

"Thank you, too, cat," Justin said, causing the cat's smile to become even wider.

The taller girl was looking intently at the carriage. "Oh, oh."

The smaller girl followed her gaze. "You're right. The rest of them are coming."

"Who's coming?" Justin asked anxiously. "What's

going on?"

As if in response to his questions, the carriage door flew off its hinges, and ghoul after ghoul began pouring out. For a few seconds, the scene reminded him of a circus in which numerous clowns emerged from a car that seemed too small to hold so many persons.

However, there was nothing humorous nor entertaining about the creatures coming from this carriage. Many of the dark-robed ghouls carried scythes and looked like death incarnate.

Some of the ghouls floated up above the buildings and hovered there, watching and waiting.

The carriage exploded, and hundreds of ghouls came flying out.

Upon seeing so many of their enemies, the smaller girl frowned. "This is more than even our kitty cat can handle. It is an entire legion. We will need to leave."

The ghouls quickly moved into positions as they attempted to encircle Justin, the two girls, and the cat. However, just before the circle closed on them, the girls grabbed Justin's hands.

"This way!" the taller girl shouted.

With great speed, faster than Justin realized that he could run, they dashed through a narrow opening. They bolted down a side street with a howling legion of ghouls in pursuit.

"This road leads out of town!" Justin declared as he ran.

Several ghouls with scythes got close enough to strike at them, but the giant cat destroyed them before the ghouls could cause any harm.

"Look! Up in the sky!" Justin shouted and pointed toward hundreds of bats that were steadily getting nearer.

The bats swirled in formation as they prepared to attack. Justin recalled an incident that his mother had told him about her childhood. While attending an outdoor musical at the Muny Opera in Forest Park, a bat had become entangled in her hair. Since that evening, his mother had always been afraid of bats. For the first time, Justin truly understood her aversion to those creatures.

The bats somehow remained equidistant from each other while they wove a V-shaped formation. He had occasionally seen large flocks of birds maintain formation as they flew in patterns that were beautiful in their harmony.

Tonight, though, he saw no beauty in the bats that now descended in the V-shaped formation like an arrow heading toward them.

"This way!" the taller girl declared.

They dashed out of the city and across an open valley. They were apparently trapped in a vise with ghouls closing in from behind them and bats closing in from in front of them.

"Ignore the bats," the smaller girl advised Justin. "They can't harm you."

The swarm of bats washed over them like an ocean wave. Justin covered his face with his hands. Over the next thirty seconds, he felt dozens of bats bounce off of his hands and body. The girls kept hold of his arms, so he continued running, trusting them to guide him safely.

"They're gone," the taller girl said.

Justin uncovered his face. They were passing groves of mulberry and sycamore trees.

When he glanced back, he was shocked to see more ghouls had joined the pursuit. Some were on foot, some flying just a few feet above the ground, and some rode carriages similar to the one that had wrecked.

"Up the hill!" the smaller girl directed them.

They dashed up a hillside covered with olive trees. The howls of the ghouls became louder and more frenzied in anticipation of catching their prey.

Upon reaching the top of the hill, they saw a wondrous sight that caused them to stop, their deadly pursuers momentarily forgotten.

A small boy in a white tunic was standing near some olive trees. At first it appeared to Justin that the boy was holding a heart-shaped object that was burning with great intensity. However, the fire did not consume the heart.

Brilliant red and white beams of light radiated from the burning heart. Then Justin realized that the boy was not holding anything.

The child's hands were held chest high as though in a welcoming gesture. The light emanated from the child's heart, which was visible in his chest.

For a few moments, Justin stood transfixed by the vision. All concerns were forgotten. Then he remembered the ghouls and looked back, half-expecting them to pounce upon him.

Justin intuitively realized that this young boy was on their side. Justin assumed that this boy was an exceptional being like the two girls. However, even with the boy's help, they still seemed hopelessly outnumbered by the legion of ghouls.

Justin realized that they were not ordinary girls, and this was certainly not an ordinary boy, but merely adding one more of their kind to the fight surely could not make that much difference.

"What are we going to do?" he asked in despair as the forces of darkness entered the garden of olive trees.

The smaller girl tilted her face upward and looked directly into his eyes. "We stand in the presence of infinite light. It is time for you to see."

"The ghouls ..." Justin stammered.

"The ghouls are powerless against him," the taller girl assured Justin. "He has intervened directly. Blessed be the child who is the Light."

Justin looked back toward the boy. The light beams emanating from his radiant heart became so intense that the night became day. The legion of ghouls vanished like a moth in a flame.

"Blessed be the Lord of the Dawn, the Prince of the Morning," the smaller girl said.

The light that engulfed them revealed new colors and previously-unseen details in everything around them -- in every tree, in every blade of grass, in every rock. He looked with wonder at the flawless beauty of the two girls.

As he looked back toward the boy, Justin was overwhelmed by the intensity of the experience, and he awoke with a start.

He sat bolt upright in bed, his heart racing.

"Wow!" he exclaimed before collapsing back onto the mattress, trying to understand the whole experience.

During the summer before his senior year in college, Justin's grandfather moved to Florida. Justin's grandmother had passed away the previous year, and his grandfather decided that he would like to live in a retirement community on the Gulf coast.

The grandfather's house was for sale, and he asked Justin to live in the house until the real estate agent found a buyer. Justin would mow the lawn, rake the leaves, shovel the snow, and do any other tasks necessary to keep the property in good condition.

Besides helping out his grandfather, this arrangement worked well for Justin because the house was within walking distance of the university. The house was also close to the home warehouse store where Justin worked as an assistant manager.

Justin hoped that everything would continue to go along peacefully and pleasantly. It did not occur to him that the gift of the beatific vision had made him a prime target of demonic forces.

Part 2

The Day of the Girl with the Broken Heart

It was a place of gold and of fire and of music that seemed to flow from some deep wellspring. The music was not loud, but it still reverberated through the church.

As the congregation exited, Philomena paused in the aisle and looked around. *What church is this? I have never been here previously.* She looked up at the shining, colorful stained glass windows depicting the Mysteries of Light, the most recent additions to the rosary.

Beautiful, she reflected, *but I don't know how I got here.* At that moment, she realized that her mother was standing next to her. Philomena's mother, Hannah, was lovely, petite, delicate.

Philomena was also small and slender. Her brown hair was in a short, pixie-like style and her brown eyes were warm and perceptive.

Hannah was holding a palm branch, an ivy leaf, and two arrows, which she handed to Philomena.

Philomena took everything that Hannah gave her. "I

23

don't understand, Mother. What is the purpose of these items?"

"They are gifts from the saint for your journey, dear," Hannah said.

Philomena looked around. "Where is father?"

"He is where he wants to be," Hannah replied.

Well, that's certainly ambiguous enough, Philomena reflected.

However, before she could ask a follow-up question, Hannah said, "We only have a few seconds, Philomena. Look for the man with the stone and the sword."

Good grief, she thought with exasperation. What does that mean?

Suddenly, she had an insight into the situation.

"Is this a dream?"

"Yes," her mother replied. "And you're waking up."

Philomena woke up in her bed in her condominium. That was unusual, she reflected. I seldom remember my dreams, but this one is still vivid in my mind.

She looked at her hands, half-expecting to see that she was still holding the palm branch, the ivy leaf, and the two arrows, but her hands were empty. I suppose that they were spiritual gifts, she reasoned.

Then she remembered something else that Hannah had said. The stone and the sword -- perhaps she meant the sword in the stone like in the Camelot legend. Maybe I'm going to marry King Arthur. Hmmm. Maybe not.

Philomena's alarm clock went off, and she silenced it, got up, and began to get ready for work. It was only 4:00 a.m., but Philomena worked in a bakery and needed to be there by 5:00 a.m. in order to have the donuts and Danishes ready for the morning customers.

Philomena enjoyed the half-mile walk to work. She moved with a fluid grace along the path that ran through a park. Few persons were outside that early in the morning. Everything was so quiet and peaceful. The chirping birds welcomed the dawn.

Philomena felt like she had the world to herself. Occasionally she encountered a jogger or walker, but they did not pay any attention to her, which was fine with her.

She worked at the bakery six days a week, and she liked the structured schedule of her workdays. On Sundays she went to the earliest Mass at 6:00 a.m. since that was consistent with her routine, and there were fewer persons at that early Mass. She wished that there was a 5:00 a.m. Mass, but no churches in her town had services that early.

Philomena preferred to remain in the kitchen during her entire shift. However, she occasionally had to go out front to the counter to wait on customers. If one of her coworkers was sick or on vacation, Philomena had to interact with the customers. Most persons were nice to her, but she still was nevertheless uncomfortable talking to customers.

Philomena's favorite duty in the bakery was making cakes and cupcakes. More precisely, she loved decorating them. As a teenager, one of her favorite television shows had been *Cupcake Wars* in which chefs competed against each other. The chef who created the most imaginatively-designed cupcake was declared the winner. Philomena never missed an episode of the show.

At her present job, she borrowed some ideas from the show such as an outer space theme with stars and planets, spaceships and astronauts. That had been a winning design for a St. Louis chef.

However, most of the designs of Philomena's cakes and cupcakes came from her own imagination. Over the past two years some of her themes had included skiers on a snowy mountain, a mermaid of a beach with seashells, a fairytale castle, the Easter Bunny hiding eggs, and Santa and his elves at the North Pole.

Just as Philomena was taking a tray of donuts out of the fryer, Audrey Pace, the owner of the bakery came in the door. Audrey was a jovial woman in her mid-sixties. To Philomena, she seemed the perfect image of what Philomena imagined Mrs. Santa Claus was like.

"Good morning, Philomena," Audrey greeted her. "How are you today, dear?"

"Fine, Mrs. Pace. How are you?"

"I'm fine, dear, but on my way here, Katie called me. She's sick. She thinks that she caught that flu that's going around."

"Oh."

"Philomena, I know that you don't enjoy being out at the counter, but I'm going to need you out there for a while today. Later today I need to go over to the bank, so you'll need to hold down the fort while I'm gone."

"That's fine."

"Really?"

"Yes, it's okay," Philomena assured her.

Audrey waited until 10:00 a.m. to go to the bank. The bakery usually had few customers between 10:00 a.m. to 11:00 a.m., so Audrey decided this would be the least stressful time to leave Philomena by herself.

Indeed, for the first fifteen minutes, there were no customers. Then, at 10:15 a.m., a young man came through the front door.

At that moment, Philomena was bending over as she placed a tray of cookies into the display case. She looked up at the man and dropped the tray, the cookies scattering on the floor.

"Oh, my goodness!" she declared.

Justin hurried forward. "Let me help you. I'm sorry if I startled you."

"It's my fault. I'm a clumsy oaf." She did not look at him, keeping her eyes on the cookies that she hastily placed back on the tray.

"No, you're not. We all drop things from time to time." He smiled at her. "I've never seen you before. Are you new here?"

"No, I've worked here for three years, but I'm usually back in the kitchen," she said, avoiding eye contact with him, but then adding with a slight grin, "I don't drop as many things when I'm in the kitchen."

"Well, these cookies still look delicious to me. And I came here specifically to get some cookies. I'll buy all the ones from that tray."

"They were on the floor!" Philomena was surprised. "They're germy!"

"Before I eat them, I'll warm them up in my microwave. That will kill any germs."

At that moment, the front door opened and Audrey entered.

Justin turned toward her. "Hi, Mrs. Pace."

"Hello."

"Mrs. Pace, I dropped this tray of cookies, and this nice man offered to buy them."

"That won't be necessary, Justin. I'm fairly sure that we can find you some clean cookies."

"I need to get a cake out of the oven before it burns," Philomena said and quickly retreated into the kitchen.

"I would be happy to buy those cookies." Justin nodded toward the tray on the counter.

"You must consider me to be a very mean person. Do you think that I'm going to fire that young lady?"

Justin chuckled. "I guess not."

"My goodness, that girl has already disappeared back into the kitchen. She is so shy! In any case, Sir Galahad, you don't have to worry: her job is secure, and I'm going to get you some fresh cookies."

Justin smiled. "This is truly my fortunate day."

Several days later, on a Sunday afternoon, Philomena walked on a hiking and biking path that ran beneath some thin woodland canopy. She was delighted when she spotted a red-winged blackbird gliding through some hickory trees.

Philomena noticed a robin searching for berries in a holly tree. Off in the distance, she could hear a woodpecker hard at work.

The path went downhill slightly toward a pond where two western painted turtles on a log basked in the sun. Some geese descended onto the pond, adding to the beauty of the day.

Philomena decided to explore a different route than she usually took. She went down a path that ran parallel to the homes on Lakeview Way.

There were many dragonflies around; they seemed to like the bright sunshine. She also spotted an Eastern bluebird.

Pleased with her walk, Philomena was about to loop back to the main path and head home. However, in the backyard of one of the homes, she noticed a young man who seemed to be hard at work on some project. Curious, she decided to venture closer to see what he was doing.

She stood behind a mulberry bush as she watched the man place red stone blocks in a circular formation around a three-foot wide steel bowl. Philomena quickly realized that he was building a fire pit.

When the man turned to pick up another stone, she got a better look at his face, and she recognized him instantly -- he was the man who had been in the bakery a few days earlier.

For twenty minutes, she intently watched him work,

unsure of why she was so drawn to the scene. She realized that it was going to take him quite a while to get all those stones precisely positioned. I suppose that I should get going again, Philomena told herself. However, she remained where she was, watching in a dream-like trance.

Then, as he lifted one of the last two stones, he happened to look up toward the mulberry bush. His glance jolted Philomena back to a state of alertness.

He squinted as he tried to discern the form behind the bush, then took a couple of steps in her direction.

"Hello?" he called to her.

Philomena blushed, then panicked and fled back onto the trail, and she ran until she was out of breath. Philomena leaned against a tree for support.

I hope that he didn't recognize me, she thought anxiously. He would think that I was some sort of crazy, stalker person. Why did I stay there watching for so long?

She resumed her trek down the trail when an idea hit her like a rock -- stones, stones -- stone -- the sword in the stone.

"Look for the man with the stone and the sword." -- That was what my mother said to me in that dream. I still have not figured out whether it was a simple dream from my subconscious or whether my mother actually sent me a message from Heaven. Will I ever determine whether it was a dream or a vision?

Could that man be the one to whom my mother was referring? He certainly had plenty of stones, but I did not see any sword.

Philomena knew that she should probably just walk home. However, compelled by some intuition, she turned around and walked back down the trail toward the yard of the man building the fire pit.

As Justin completed his work on the fire pit, he glanced up the hill at the mulberry bush. A few minutes earlier he had noticed a woman standing behind the bush, but she had run away when he called out to her.

Although Justin had not gotten a good look at the woman, she seemed familiar to him. He realized that the trail was popular with walkers, joggers, and cyclists, so he supposed that it was probable that persons that he knew would occasionally pass by his yard.

That woman who ran away certainly did not want to

talk to me, though, he reflected with a wry grin. Just like that young woman in the bakery, she couldn't get away from me fast enough. I must have the opposite of a magnetic personality.

Justin placed a starter log on the fire pit grate, then stacked a few wood logs over the starter log, which he then lit. As soon as the fire started steadily burning, he covered the fire pit with the screen lid.

Justin sat down in an Adirondack chair and watched the fire.

While he was enjoying the results of his work, Justin again saw movement up by the mulberry bush. The woman had returned.

He stood up and waved to her. "Hi!"

She hesitated, and for a second, he thought that she was going to run away again. She seemed as skittish as a deer.

On this occasion, though, she walked around the bush and gracefully descended the small hill into the yard. Because he had just thought of her a short while ago, Justin recognized her instantly.

"That's a nice trail," he greeted her. "I often take

walks on it myself."

"Yes, it's one of my favorite places," she agreed. She blushed and looked at the ground.

"A few days ago at the bakery, I was speaking with either you or your twin sister," Justin said, trying to use humor to relax her.

Philomena laughed and looked at him. "Oh, you were talking to me. Mrs. Pace doesn't allow my twin sister into the bakery; my sister eats too many doughnuts and cookies."

Justin chuckled. "That seems reasonable."

"Mrs. Pace is very reasonable person. I like working in her bakery."

"Except for those days when strange men seeking cookies come in?" Justin grinned broadly.

Philomena laughed. "Yes, I like working in the bakery -- except for those strange, cookie-seeking men."

"I'd like to return to the subject of your twin sister. With twins there always has to be a good one and a bad one. Which one are you?"

"I'm definitely the good one."

"I'm glad to hear it." He paused, then added,

"However, the bad twin would claim to be the good one."

She laughed. "That's true."

"I guess that I'll just have to hope for the best. What is your name?"

"Philomena."

"That's a very pretty name. I have never previously met anyone named Philomena."

"My mother chose the name," she said enthusiastically. "Philomena means 'daughter of light.' I am named after Saint Philomena, who was a young Greek princess. Her father was a king in Greece. When he took his family to Rome to ask for peace, the Emperor Diocletian wanted Philomena to be his wife, but she refused. Diocletian was furious and tried to drown Philomena with an anchor tied to her. However, two angels cut the rope and placed her safely on a riverbank."

"That's great!"

"And there's more! On three occasions, Diocletian had his archers try to kill Philomena, but on the first attempt, her wounds were healed; on the second attempt, the arrows appeared to be deflected away from her and missed her; and on the third attempt, the arrows boomeranged back and killed some of the archers. Later, several of the surviving archers became Christians."

"Philomena certainly had some excellent defenders working on her behalf," Justin said.

"Yes. Philomena was eventually martyred, but she completed her work in this world."

"You were named after a great saint," Justin said. "Does everyone call you 'Philomena' or do you have a nickname?"

"A nickname?"

"Like Philly or something? What do your friends call you?"

"Umm." She hesitated and looked at the ground.

Justin immediately regretted asking the question. Based on her reaction she did not have any friends, and she did not want him to know.

"That's okay," he said hastily. "I don't have a nickname either. Everyone just calls me 'Justin.' Philomena is such a good name that it should be left just like it is."

"Thank you." She glanced over at the fire pit. "You did a wonderful job building your fire pit. You already have a nice fire burning in it!"

"Thanks," Justin said. "Recently I noticed that they have begun springing up around town, so I decided to build one of my own. As is often the case, I didn't know what I was doing, so I watched some how-to-build-a-fire-pit videos. The videos were very helpful."

"I'm glad that it turned out so well." Philomena started to walk back toward the hill. "It's been wonderful talking to you, but I'd better be on my way."

"Oh, okay. It was great talking to you, too."

"I hope to see you in the bakery again soon. Next time I'll try not to spill all of your cookies onto the floor."

Justin laughed. "And I'll keep on guard against your evil twin! Bye!"

"See you!"

Philomena almost skipped up the hill and onto the trail. As he watched her, Justin thought that it was fitting that she was named after a princess. Her pixie-haircut, lithe figure, and mincing steps brought into his mind the image of an elf princess gliding through the woods.

Two days later Justin went into the bakery. As he

spoke with Audrey Pace, Philomena emerged from the kitchen. Audrey was surprised to see her because Philomena usually wanted as little contact with customers as possible.

"Hi, Justin," she said cheerfully.

"Good afternoon, Philomena."

"Actually, I'm her twin sister -- Fiona. Philomena was sick today, so I'm substituting for her."

"Then how do you know my name?"

"Okay, you caught me! I'm Philomena -- the good one -- I'm always good."

"I believe you."

"This is very confusing!" Audrey declared with a grin. She was pleased that Philomena had developed such a good repertoire with Justin, who was one of Audrey's favorite customers.

"Justin and I are just crazy, Mrs. Pace."

"Well, I have some cakes that I need to get out of the oven, so I'll leave you two crazy persons alone." Audrey discretely went back into the kitchen in order to give them some privacy.

"Mrs. Pace is so sweet," Philomena said.

"She is," Justin agreed.

"It looks like you bought plenty of cookies today." Philomena said, looking at the box on the counter.

"Yes, but I'll likely be back in a couple of days. For some reason, this place seems to draw me toward it like a magnet."

Philomena giggled. "You're silly."

Justin nodded toward the store's large front window. "Before I came inside, I was trying to guess which of the cars out front was yours. None of them seemed quite right for you, though."

"You are absolutely correct because none of those cars belong to me. I don't own a car. In fact, I don't even have a driver's license."

Justin was somewhat surprised by this information. "Why not?"

"My father always discouraged me from learning to drive. He said that he could drive me anywhere that I needed to go. My mother had a driver's license, but he didn't really didn't like her driving much either. He was very protective of us. My father was a very good man."

Justin noticed her use of the past tense. "Have your

parents passed away, Philomena?" he asked gently.

She looked at the floor. "Yes. My father's been gone for two years and my mother for four years. She worked in the flower shop down the street."

"What did your father do?"

"Oh, he had a lot of different jobs," she said evasively. "He didn't like most of his supervisors. They treated him very unfairly. After a year or two at a job, he'd either quit or get fired."

"I see."

"I might as well tell you something now and get it out of the way." Philomena sounded nervous. "My mother was murdered four years ago. She went missing for a few days, and then the police found her body in farmer's field just outside of town."

"I'm so sorry, Philomena," Justin said.

"The police and a lot of persons around town thought that my father had killed her, but of course, he didn't. He had a bit of a temper, but he would never have killed anyone, especially not my mother. Personally, I have always suspected that a drifter passing through town abducted my mother and murdered her. The farmer told the police that he had seen a suspicious-looking man walking along the road near the field. The farmer did not get a close look at the man, but his description did not match my father at all."

"The drifter could have been some sort of psychopath," Justin said, knowing that this was what Philomena wanted to believe.

"Right," Philomena said. "Anyway, because he was the prime suspect, my father was treated like a leper around town. He stayed home during the day, then went out at night to socialize with his friends at a bar. Unfortunately, one night about two years ago, he got into a fight at a bar and got stabbed to death."

"Philomena, you are such a nice person, and you have suffered so much," Justin said, placing a consoling hand on her shoulder. "We all have a cross to carry, but yours is especially heavy."

"Thank you, Justin. I loved my mother very much -- and my father, too, of course. He wasn't much for conversation, but he didn't let me have any illusions about myself. He told me, 'Philomena, I'm a plainspoken man. I tell it like it is. I don't want to hurt your feelings, but you have to stop kidding yourself. You are a homely girl -- not ugly -- but you are homely.' "

"You are very pretty, Philomena," Justin objected.

"Well, he didn't think so, and I suppose that I agreed with him about my looks. I kept to myself during my years in school. My father didn't consider me to be very bright either. He told me not to worry, though. He would protect me. My father was really a very good man. He did have a temper and drinking made it worse, but he was still a good man."

He looked down at the ground, not wanting her to see in his eyes what he thought about this matter. Justin intuitively knew to keep his opinions to himself for the present time. Quickly mastering his emotions, he looked back up at Philomena.

Her eyes were sparkling. She had been watching him intently. He wondered whether on some semi-conscious level she realized the inaccuracy of her assessment of her father. Perhaps it was a lie that she told herself in order to re-invent her personal history.

In any case, Philomena seemed to appreciate his discretion.

"Thanks for being such an attentive listener. And thank you for being patient. I have been talking your ear off."

"Not at all. I enjoy a good conversation." Justin moved toward the door. "However, I don't want to annoy Mrs. Pace by keeping you from your work, so I'd better get going."

"Oh, Mrs. Pace doesn't mind," Philomena said with a grin. "And I'm almost done for the day. I get off work in a half hour."

"I was planning to go to the diner across the street to get something to eat. Would you like to join me after you get off work?"

"That would be very nice," Philomena said, surprised by the offer.

"Good. I'll see you then."

After Justin left the bakery, he ran a couple of errands, then arrived at the diner just as Philomena was crossing the street.

"Perfect timing," he said, holding the door for her as they went inside.

After sitting down in a booth near the window, they

resumed their earlier conversation while enjoying some grilled cheese sandwiches and roasted butternut squash soup.

On Saturday afternoon, Philomena and Justin rented a bicycle-built-for-two from a bike shop, then rode it on the path in the park. They stopped near the lake in order to have a picnic lunch consisting of turkey sandwiches, potato chips, and sodas. Afterwards, they fed bread crumbs to the ducks on the lake.

On Sunday evening, they went to a movie, a comedy which they both enjoyed. Then, after the movie, they stopped by the ice cream shop and had sundaes.

The next weekend they visited the planetarium, the history museum, and attended a play in the theater at the community college.

Both Philomena and Justin liked playing board games and card games. Game nights became a regular part of their weekly activities.

That September and the first half of October was an idyllic time for both Philomena and Justin.

One warm, windy Sunday afternoon in mid-October,

they flew kites in the park. After about an hour, they decided to take a break and sat down on a bench.

"I'm looking forward to Halloween," Philomena said. "It's only ten days away."

"Yep."

"I have always liked Halloween a lot because I could hide myself in some wonderful costume," Philomena declared with bubbly enthusiasm. "During the years that I went trick-or-treating, I almost always dressed as a fairy tale princess. On that one evening, I could pretend to be beautiful. I hoped that somehow the pretense would become a reality."

"Well, you succeeded beyond your wildest dreams," Justin said.

"If I'm beautiful to you, that's the important thing."

"Philomena, when people see us together, they are reminded of a fairy tale -- Beauty and the Beast."

"Oh, you're so silly!" she laughed. "So what did you dress as for Halloween?"

"I went as a knight a couple of times."

"That was appropriate -- you're my knight in shining armor."

"Thank you, my princess."

"What other costumes did you wear?"

"I only went trick-or-treating two or three times when I was a very little boy. Then I began to have awful nightmares. The nightmares occurred all throughout the year, but some of the more gruesome Halloween imagery seemed to make the nightmares worse. My parents also kept me away from haunted houses and horror movies."

"That's unfortunate. Halloween can be fun."

"Yes. As it turned out, Halloween really wasn't the problem."

She looked at him intently. "What was the problem?"

Justin sighed. "You will probably think that I'm crazy and run away."

"No, I won't," she encouraged him. "Tell me everything."

"All right." Justin told her everything about the demon who had attempted to possess him, about the two supernatural girls who helped him, and about the boy with a heart of fire who saved them all.

Later that night, Philomena tossed and turned in bed. She had so many thoughts going through her mind that she found it difficult to sleep. Philomena believed Justin's story. She was a religious person who believed in the spiritual dimension. Philomena was open to the possibility of supernatural events occurring. It seemed that Justin had experienced the ultimate spiritual reality.

At least she was certain that he believed every word that he told her. She was certain that Justin was a very good man. He was the best man that she had ever known. As a result of knowing Justin, Philomena was now able to see her father in a clearer light.

Reality Check -- Bradley Marr, my father, was a troubled man with a bad temper. He was abusive toward me and my mother -- in fact, he probably murdered her. And his bad temper ultimately got him killed when he encountered another man as mean as he was. However, he was still my father and, in spite of the bad things that he said and did, I still feel love for him and will continue to pray for him. Can my prayers still help him?

Philomena recalled something said in a recent sermon by her parish priest. "God exists outside of time, so the past, present, and future are all equally present to God at every moment." So I suppose my prayers can help those long dead as well as those persons who have not yet been born. Perhaps I should pray for my future children -- if I have any. If I am a mother someday, I hope that I am as good a mother as my own mother.

With that thought, Philomena drifted back into sleep and slept peacefully for the rest of the night.

It was late afternoon on Halloween, and Justin was preparing to leave the house. He wanted to be out of there before the trick-or-treaters began showing up at the front door. He knew that the children would get plenty of candy from the other houses in the neighborhood, so it was not necessary for him to participate.

Philomena's enthusiasm for Halloween had helped him to look at this holiday more positively, but it had not been a complete paradigm shift. If Philomena and I get married someday, we will receive trick-or-treaters into our home, Justin reflected, but until that time, I'm going to continue to skip this holiday.

Will we be married next year at this time? Justin

wondered how long he should wait to propose to her. He felt certain that Philomena was the right woman for him to marry, and he hoped that she felt the same way. However, he did not want to make the mistake of proposing too soon. Sometime next year would be fine, he reasoned -- perhaps on Valentine's Day.

Justin suddenly realized that it was starting to get dark outside. He had planned to be gone before dusk, before any trick-or-treaters began going down his street.

Just as he reached for his car keys, the doorbell rang. He groaned and tried to decide whether to open the door. *I should have left fifteen minutes ago,* Justin reprimanded himself. *Now what? I don't have any candy for these kids. I suppose that I could just give them some money.*

The doorbell rang again. He walked toward to door, somewhat annoyed. *I did not turn on the porch light. Why are they ringing the bell?*

He opened the door to see a vampire, a werewolf, and a zombie looking up at him expectantly.

"Trick or treat!" the three boys called out in unison.

Justin was momentarily distracted, though. He looked with surprise at the porch light, which was glowing brightly. The porch light was on.

"Trick or treat," one of the boys repeated.

"Oh, yeah." Justin returned his attention to the boys. He pulled out his wallet, unsure of how much money he had in it. There were three twenty dollar bills and three five dollar bills. "Here you go, guys," he said, handing a five dollar bill to each of the boys.

"Thanks!" the werewolf said enthusiastically.

"Thank you, Mister," the zombie called back as he and his friends headed toward the next house. "I like your light display!"

"My light display?" Justin asked mystified.

As his neighbors greeted the three boys, Justin walked outside to the front sidewalk. His mouth fell open as he looked back at his house. Numerous strands of orange, black, and yellow lights outlined the windows, porch, and roof of the house. Every few seconds the light pattern changed from chasing to blinking to twinkling. A large, illuminated Jack-o-Lantern light sculpture was on the roof.

"Good grief!" Justin declared.

He tried to figure out from where the decorations

had come. Obviously someone is playing a joke on me, he reasoned. Almost everyone who knows me well knows that I don't like Halloween. Whoever did this certainly went to a lot of trouble for a joke. It is kind of funny, he had to admit to himself.

Could Philomena have done this? This situation would appeal to her sense of humor, but a practical joke like this doesn't seem like her style, and I can't picture her up on the roof stringing lights and placing that Jack-o-Lantern there. Who else could have done it?

And how could they have done it so quickly and so silently? Even though this is a one-story house, they would have needed to use a ladder to get those decorations on the roof. I was sitting in a chair in the living room, but I didn't hear anything.

Justin's speculations were interrupted by the arrival of the next group of trick-or-treaters. Alice in Wonderland, Cinderella, and Little Red Riding Hood came skipping along the front sidewalk.

"Hi girls," he welcomed them. "I am going to have to go back inside to get something for you."

Justin thought that he only had three twenty dollar

bills remaining in his wallet. However, as he stepped back inside, he checked his wallet and found that he had three five dollar bills in it along with the three twenties.

I must have overlooked those additional five dollar bills, he decided.

He gave five dollars to each of the girls as they stood in the doorway.

"Can I have a Snickers bar?" the girl dressed as Cinderella asked.

"Ellie, the man already gave us money," the girl in the Alice in Wonderland costume scolded her friend.

"I'm sorry, but I don't have any ..." Justin's words trailed off as he followed the girls' eyes, which were focused on a large bowl of candy on the hallway table.

"Are you okay, Mister?"

"I'm fine. I didn't think that I had any candy, but obviously I do. Help yourselves, girls."

The girls eagerly took from the bowl some Milky Way bars, Snickers, Butterfingers, Peanut Butter Cups, and other candies. They thanked Justin, then hurried toward the next house.

Justin quickly turned off the porch light and the

Halloween decorative lights. He picked up the candy bowl and examined it. This is even more mysterious than the outdoor lights.

He did not have much time to speculate about the source of the candy. The doorbell rang again.

Justin sighed and opened the door. The porch light and decorative lights were shining brightly.

"Trick-or-treat!" seven children exclaimed.

The Green Lantern, Captain America, Spiderman, Batman, Batgirl, Superman, and Supergirl stood at his door.

"Seven superheroes," Justin commented. "This neighborhood is certainly well-protected this evening."

"Right!" the 12-year-old Batman agreed.

"Take as much candy as you want," Justin said, holding the bowl forward for the children.

After they had filled their bags, the children departed. Justin's eyes widened as he noticed a new addition to his front yard. A giant, inflatable black cat that was almost 8-feet high was in the middle of the lawn. Its broad smile reminded him of another giant black cat that he had seen years ago.

Justin could not understand what was happening. It seemed like a dream, but he was certain that he was awake. He could not conceive of any logical explanation. He stared into the face of the inflatable black cat, which grinned at him like a Cheshire cat.

Two more trick-or-treaters approached. Seeing the two girls, he retreated back into the house to get some candy for them.

He looked down to see a little, blond-haired girl and an older, taller girl with brown hair. They wore similar sparkling costumes that he supposed were illuminated by fiber optics.

"You can have all of the remaining candy, girls," he said as he presented the bowl to them. "I'm leaving, so you are my final trick-or-treaters this evening."

"But your house is so pretty, Justin!" the smaller girl said.

"And doesn't that big black cat on your lawn remind you of our kitty cat?" the taller girl added.

At that instant, Justin recognized the two girls. He became momentarily light-headed as he tried to reconcile the merger of the dream world with the real world.

"Am I dreaming?" he asked.

"No, we are here in the physical world," the smaller girl said. "There is much here that needs to be done."

"And we need to get started this evening," the taller girl said.

"It's good to see both of you again," he said. "At least now I know that I'm not going crazy. I assume that the two of you are responsible for all the outdoor decorations, for the porch light going on, for the bowl of candy, and for the additional money in my wallet."

"We did it all," the taller girl acknowledged. "We were trying to get you into the spirit of the day."

"I don't like Halloween," Justin said flatly. "The two of you should understand why."

"This is the eve of two wonderful holy days -- the Feast of All Souls and the Feast of All Saints. It is a time to celebrate the communion of saints."

"Justin, you need to become more actively involved in the world," the smaller girl added. "You can't achieve your mission by hiding in the backroom of a dark house."

"It is a time for action and active engagement," the taller girl said.

"Engagement in more ways than one," the smaller girl said with a cheerful grin.

"What does that mean?" Justin asked.

"You'll see," she said enigmatically.

"That's what I'm afraid of."

"Be not afraid."

"It's time for the next of your Halloween surprises," the taller girl declared.

"What is it?"

"If we told you …"

"It wouldn't be a surprise," he completed the sentence for her.

"That is correct. Now it is your turn to go trick-or-treating."

"You're kidding."

" 'Kidding' is not inherent to our nature," the taller girl said. Her tone reminded Justin that he was not dealing with children, despite their appearance.

"All right." He felt certain that it was best to go along with whatever they advised.

"Come with us," the small blonde said.

Justin and his two companions walked five blocks to

their first destination. He supposed that their trio appeared to be a young father taking his two daughters trick-or-treating.

The girls stopped in front of a small, dilapidated house that was in need of painting and many other repairs.

"You are going reverse trick-or-treating, Justin," the taller girl declared cheerfully.

"What is reverse trick-or-treating?" Justin asked.

"Instead of receiving something from each place that you visit, you are going to give something," the smaller girl explained. "We are going to take you to visit persons who are desperately poor, and you are going to give them money."

"I don't have much money, and I have very little money with me," he objected.

"We will see to it that you have what you need to do your good deeds."

"How?"

"You certainly ask a lot of questions, Justin," the smaller girl said.

He was about to ask another question, then decided that silence was the wiser way to proceed. Justin walked up onto the front porch on which a porch light was illuminated. Justin wondered whether the homeowners had turned on the porch light or whether the girls had done so like they did at his own home.

He knocked on the front door, and a few seconds later, an elderly woman opened the door. A smile brightened her face upon seeing the two girls and their "father." She was held out a bowl of candy for the girls.

"Oh, you two are positively adorable!" she bubbled. Noticing that each girl only took one candy bar, the woman added, "Take some more candy, girls!"

"Actually, we are here to give you something," the taller girl said, inconspicuously nudging Justin with her elbow.

"Yes," Justin began hesitatingly. "That's right. . . .We call it reverse trick-or-treating. I have recently been blessed financially, so I want to help other persons. I'm giving money to other persons in the community, and I wanted to give money to you."

He opened his wallet, having no idea how much money was inside. It was almost bursting at the seams with hundred dollar bills. Justin glanced down at the girls, unsure whether he was supposed to give all this money to this elderly woman or whether that money needed to last for the entire evening. The girls just smiled at him without giving him any clue how to proceed.

Justin decided to error on the side of generosity. He took all the money out of the wallet and handed it to the startled woman.

"How much money is here?" she asked flabbergasted. The woman felt that it would be inappropriate to count the money at this moment.

"I honestly have no idea," Justin admitted. "Whatever amount is there is the amount that I want you to have and that you are supposed to have. Happy Halloween!"

As he began backing away from the doorway, he noticed tears welling up in the woman's eyes. "Thank you so much!" she exclaimed. "You have no idea how much I needed this money -- or perhaps you do know! God bless you!"

"Thanks! God bless you, too!" Justin called as he and the girls returned to the sidewalk and continued down the street.

They went to dozens of homes that evening. They also visited numerous homeless persons living in alleys or under highway overpasses. Justin lost track of how much money he gave away that evening, but he was certain that it had to be over two hundred thousand dollars.

Everyone -- from children to elderly persons -- was grateful and astonished by the generosity of this mysterious young man who appeared out of nowhere, then vanished into the night.

They seemed to travel from site to site almost instantly. After seemingly spending many hours reverse trick-or-treating, Justin sat down on the steps of the apartment building from which they had just visited two apartments.

"I'm exhausted," he remarked.

The smaller girl touched his shoulder and instantly his energy level was completely replenished. He felt like he had just enjoyed a long sleep and a good meal.

"Thank you for that energy boost and for sending me on this mission this evening. I have given away a lot of money tonight, but I'm the one who feels like a million dollars." He stood up. "Let's head to the next destination."

"You did well, Justin," the taller girl commended him. "Our evening's mission is complete."

Justin nodded. "It must be very late. I'm surprised that persons are still opening their doors when we knock; it must be after midnight by now." He glanced at the time on his cell phone, and his eyes widened upon seeing that it was only eight o'clock. "This can't be correct!"

"The time on your phone is correct," the smaller girl said.

"How did we go so far and do so much in such a short period of time?"

"Time flows differently for us, Justin."

"Within a river, currents at different depths flow at different speeds, yet all the currents flow within the same river," the taller girl said. Noticing the puzzled expression on his face, she added, "It's a bit complicated, Justin."

"Okay," he said, accepting that there were mysteries that he could not understand. "I really like this magic wallet!"

When both girls frowned at him, he amended his statement, "I really like this miraculous wallet."

"That's better," the taller girl said.

"Are we going to do this again next year or was it just a one-time thing?"

"If we need to do it next All Hallow's Eve, then we will do it."

"Don't you know?"

"We're not omniscient, Justin."

"Omniscient means having total knowledge, knowing everything," the smaller girl explained.

"Yes, I know what it means," Justin said, somewhat impatiently.

"The blank look on your face seemed to indicate otherwise," the taller girl said.

"Wow! You two don't pull your punches."

"We aren't planning to punch you."

"It's just an expression."

"I know," she replied with a slight smile.

Justin laughed, and they took him home where he soon fell into a deep sleep filled with pleasant dreams.

Even though he was an immortal spirit, the demon in a black cowl knew that he had somehow been diminished. The ghoul was not now what he once had been. That knowledge fueled the flames of rage burning within him. Causing pain, destruction, and chaos were the only things that interested him now.

He cracked the whip at the ghostly horse that pulled his carriage along a lonely road. Two hellhounds obediently followed the carriage, awaiting his commands.

I would like to go after that boy, the demon thought bitterly, but I missed my opportunity. The guardians have him too well-protected now. He is too shielded for me to attack him directly in his dreams. However, there are other roads that I can travel.

All the roads are guarded, so I will need help breaking through into the mortal world. He mystically summoned other demons, and soon other carriages rode alongside his carriage while more demons flew in the sky above them. A pack of hellhounds ran behind the carriages, eagerly anticipating many kills.

He looked with pleasure at the legion. Now I need to find a road that will take me into the mortal world. Then I will find a way to destroy the boy and those whom he loves.

On Thanksgiving Day, Justin set the silverware and prepared the place settings on his dining room table. Philomena was going to come over later that day for dinner.

Justin checked on the turkey roasting in the oven, then began to prepare some mashed potatoes.

Suddenly, the smaller girl appeared at his left side. "What's for dessert?" she asked, looking up at him.

"Hey!" Justin was startled. "I'm not accustomed to having someone pop out of thin air into my kitchen."

"You shouldn't be so nervous, Justin," the taller girl said, appearing on his right side. "All is well."

"I'm glad to hear it," he said. "Anyway, I'm glad to see both of you. I don't feel that I adequately thanked you after our reverse trick-or-treating adventure on Halloween. That was a great evening. I have continued to seek out persons to help. My wallet no longer miraculously generates cash, but I try to do what I can with my limited funds."

"Excellent," the smaller girl said. "Keep up the good work, Justin."

"I will."

"Our visit this afternoon will be brief, Justin. The enemy is attacking on many fronts, and we must go to prepare a counterstrike."

"But before we leave, we want to prompt you into action," the taller girl said. "You have a tendency to procrastinate."

Justin sighed. "Okay. What am I supposed to do?"

"Propose marriage to Philomena."

His eyes widened. "I was planning to propose to her someday. However, I thought that I should wait a while longer. I have only known her for about three months."

"The time is now. I would recommend proposing this evening."

"I need to purchase an engagement ring, and there aren't any jewelry stores open on Thanksgiving Day."

"You can give her your grandmother's engagement ring. You are her only grandchild, and she would want Philomena to have it."

"I agree," Justin said. "In fact, she mentioned to me on several occasions that she wanted my future wife to have that ring. However, I don't know where the ring is.

Before he moved to Florida, my grandfather and I searched for the ring, but we couldn't find it. My grandmother worried about burglars, so she would find clever hiding places for her money and more expensive jewelry."

"The ring is in a jewelry box on the top shelf in the hallway closet," the smaller girl said.

"I looked for it in that jewelry box, but it wasn't there," Justin objected.

"The box has a false bottom that conceals a hidden compartment. The ring is in that hidden compartment."

"Thanks. Are you sure that you're not omniscient?"

"Quite."

At that moment, the attention of both girls clearly went elsewhere. They heard some voice that Justin could not hear or saw some vision that he could not see.

"We must leave immediately," the taller girl told him. "The enemy forces are in the field, and the hellhounds are howling."

"Farewell for now, Justin," the smaller girl said. "Give our love to Philomena."

Instantly, they were gone. Justin reflected upon what they had just said. He hoped that their battle against evil went well.

Justin went down the hallway and got the jewelry box from the top shelf of the hallway closet. He quickly found the box's false bottom and took out his grandmother's engagement ring. The ring had a rather small diamond, but its sentimental value to him was priceless.

Philomena arrived about twenty minutes later. She brought a pumpkin pie that she had made at the bakery. It was decorated with several little plastic pilgrims gathered around a little plastic turkey.

"Those are actually cake decorations, but I improvised a bit," Philomena said with a grin as she placed the pie on the dining room table.

"The pie looks very pretty -- not as pretty as the woman bringing it, but pretty nevertheless," Justin said.

"Thank you, kind sir," Philomena laughed.

They enjoyed the turkey dinner along with the dressing, mashed potatoes, and gravy. When it was time for dessert, Justin handed a plate with a slice of pie to Philomena.

"What's that on the pilgrim's head?" she asked,

looking down at the plastic decoration.

"It looks like a little halo," Justin said. "Your pilgrim must be a saint."

At that moment, Philomena realized that it was a diamond ring on the pilgrim's head.

"Oh, my goodness!" she exclaimed with wide eyes.

Justin picked up his Thanksgiving-themed napkin, which depicted a cornucopia filled with an abundant harvest of fruits and vegetables. Justin went down on one knee and read her the verse that he had written on the back of the napkin:

"Philomena, Daughter of Light,

On this Thanksgiving night,

I give thanks for your radiant life,

And I want you to be my wife.

If you will accept this diamond ring,

Great joy to me you will bring."

He handed her the poem, then added, "Philomena, I love you. Will you marry me?"

"Of course, Justin! I love you, too!"

They kissed, and she placed the ring onto her left hand.

The demonic ghoul rode in haste away from the carnage behind him. All those that he had summoned had been destroyed in the battle against the forces of Light. The legion had been utterly defeated. Looking back, he could see the shattered forms of all the demons and hellhounds that he had summoned.

The destroyed creatures vanished in the abyss, no longer of any use to him. Yet they had served their purpose: he had managed to get much closer to a gateway leading into the mortal world.

Philomena knew that something was wrong, but she could not identify the source of the disturbance. For the past week, she had been unable to sleep for more than two or three hours. She was troubled by terrible nightmares from which she awoke screaming.

She could not remember the details about the nightmares, but in her mind's eye, she saw a clear image a ghoul in a black cowl riding a carriage pulled by a ghostly horse.

From Justin's description of his nightmarish visions,

Philomena knew that this demonic figure was very similar to the demon who had pursued him. Philomena wondered whether what Justin had told her had somehow become engrained into her imagination, playing upon her own fears while she was unconscious.

Because she was getting so little sleep, every morning she went into the bakery exhausted. She managed to get through the workday, but it was difficult to do so. Philomena hoped that these nightmares would soon go away.

Although it had taken a long while and much effort, the demon in a black cowl had eventually found his way out of the abyss into which he had been cast. Riding his grim carriage along endless roads of a nightmare world, he eventually found a road that led back into the mortal world.

It was a road paved with the bad deeds of an ill-tempered man, who had unintentionally given the demon a gateway into the mortal world. With a mad, cackling laughter, the demon rode through the gateway and headed directly toward the daughter of the ill-tempered man.

Philomena dreamed that she was a princess whose room was at the top of a high tower. The animated movie *Tangled* about Rapunzel was one of her favorite films. Tonight, in her dream, Philomena found herself in a situation remarkably similar to that of the Rapunzel story.

Philomena looked out the window of her tower. To her delight, at the far end of the courtyard, she saw Justin. He was standing at the base of a large stone from which a sword protruded. Justin seemed to be contemplating the sword in the stone, probably trying to decide whether he would be able to remove the sword and claim it as his own.

Philomena was confident that he could do it. She then realized that he would need some way to reach this room at the top of the tower. Philomena willed that her short hair would become long and flowing like Rapunzel's hair. Her hair obeyed her will and flowed down the tower wall.

When she looked back across the courtyard, Justin took a step forward toward the stone. Apparently he was about to make an attempt to draw the sword.

However, at that moment, a heavy fog rolled over

the courtyard and tower. Justin and the sword and stone were completely obscured from her view.

She heard the clatter of carriage wheels on the courtyard's cobblestones. Several dogs barked loudly and angrily. This was followed by the sound of boots on the cobblestones as someone approached the tower.

She looked down to see a tall figure in a black cowl. Holding a scythe, he looked exactly like the classic image of a grim reaper. Philomena recalled Justin's story about the demon who had tormented him. She wondered whether this was the same demon.

The ghoul advanced toward her flowing hair that had extended all the way to the base of the tower in anticipation of Justin climbing the hair up to her room. Now, by an act of will, Philomena caused her hair to retract back to its normal length. She had no intention of providing a ladder for a ghoul.

His head tilted upward. Although she could not see his face, she knew that he was looking at her. Somehow she could sense that he hated her.

Perhaps he can't get to me while I'm up here, Philomena thought anxiously.

The ghoul slammed his scythe against the cobblestone courtyard and sent a powerful, reverberating shock wave into the brick tower. For a few seconds, the tower held together, but then collapsed. Thousands of bricks came crashing down.

Philomena felt herself somersaulting through the air as she fell. She landed amidst the rubble, momentarily dazed. As she struggled to her feet, Philomena realized that somehow she was not injured. This seemed mysterious, but she did not have any time to reflect upon the situation. Through the dust and fog, she could see the ghoul advancing toward her -- its scythe held high in readiness to strike.

Philomena turned and ran in the opposite direction. With long strides, the ghoul pursued her, confident that his prey would soon be caught.

In a pleasant dream, Justin was walking through a scenic woodland that reminded him of Winnie-the-Pooh's 100-acre wood. Butterflies flitted around him as he walked past some dogwood trees in full bloom and headed toward some colorful tulips. A stone bench looked like an inviting place to sit and relax. He wished that Philomena was here with him.

Suddenly, the sun was obscured behind some dark clouds, and the beautiful surroundings seemed to melt away. He found himself in the middle of a barren wasteland.

It was evident that a battle had recently occurred. The shattered remnants of numerous carriages were strewn over the road. The broken bodies of numerous ghouls, ghostly horses, and hellhounds lay in defeat all around him.

Justin then noticed the two girls standing a short distance ahead of him in the middle of the road. They waited patiently for him to adjust to his new surroundings.

"What's going on, girls?" he asked.

"We took you out of your dream because time is crucial," the smaller girl said.

"As you can see, our side won the battle here, but one of the demons got away with his four hellhounds," the taller girl added. "More demons are on the way toward the gateway, so we must remain to stop them. If they get through the gateway, they will possess and destroy many human persons. The demons must be stopped here."

"What do I need to do?" Justin asked.

"The demon who got through the gateway is going after Philomena. He is the same demon who tormented you so many times throughout the years. You must stop him."

Justin was horrified. "He's going after Philomena! I will stop him!"

"Then awake! Awake now!" the taller girl urged him.

"Go to her! Go like the wind!" the smaller girl declared.

Justin awoke and sat bolt upright. Within seconds, he was dressed and rushing out the door. He ran onto the hiking path that ran through the light woods behind his house.

He ran and ran and ran. The world seemed to take on an ethereal, mystical quality.

As Justin got near her condo, he realized that he had covered the distance much quicker than should have been possible. Somehow the girls had expedited his journey. It reminded him of his experience on Halloween when they accomplished in three hours what should have taken six or seven hours.

Apparently, he reflected, when the mortal, physical dimension unites with the spiritual dimension, we enter into a different way that time flows.

Fortunately, a few days earlier, Philomena had given Justin a key to the condo. He unlocked the door and rushed into the bedroom.

He was shocked to see her distress as her body convulsed on the bed that shook from the intensity of the attack upon her.

"Philomena!" Justin placed his hand on her shoulder and began to pray.

Within moments, Justin was hurled into the same spiritual, mystical reality that Philomena was experiencing. She was running through a woodland with the demon in close pursuit.

Justin ran toward them, intending to hurl himself at the demon, who appeared in the same ghoulish form in which he had haunted Justin's nightmares in earlier years. Justin had no idea how he could prevail in a fight against such a powerful enemy, but he knew that he had to try. I'll fight him and hope for the best, he resolved.

However, before he could reach the ghoul and Philomena, four hellhounds came bounding through the trees. They formed a line between Justin and their demon master. Although his path forward was blocked, Justin decided to try to sprint past the beasts. He realized that he might be torn apart by them, but time was running out for Philomena, and he knew that he had to try.

At that instant, the two girls appear at his side.

"Our battle is won; however, yours still needs to be fought. Continue to pray, Justin."

The smaller girl handed him a gleaming sword. "This is the sword wrought by your faith."

"With this sword, conquer," the taller girl told him just before they vanished.

Justin charged at the hellhounds. Within seconds, two of the beasts no longer had heads, and the other two strategically retreated behind some bushes.

Meanwhile, Philomena ran down a steep hill toward a lake. She hoped that he would not be able to follow her into the water. However, before she reached the lake, the ghoul caught Philomena. He seized her by the throat and pinned her to the ground.

"I am Philomena -- a daughter of light," she said defiantly. "My patron saint was martyred, but you shall not kill me."

"Kill you? I never planned to kill you. That would not be enough pleasure for me. I won't kill you. I'm going to take possession of you. I will walk the earth in your body. First, I'll exact a terrible revenge against your beloved boyfriend."

"Oh, no!"

"Oh, yes. It will be a terrible revenge. I am going to kill him. What would be the most painful way for him to die? I suppose that it doesn't much matter. The physical pain will be nothing compared to the emotional pain of seeing you kill him. How could you betray him? That is what he will wonder. As he looks into your hate-filled face, he will think that your love was just a clever deception."

"You could not deceive him. He will always recognize his evil enemy."

The demon's eyes burned with hatred. He

intensified his focus upon her as he attempted to take possession of her. Philomena resisted with all her might, but she did not know how long she could continue the fight against such a powerful creature.

Just when it seemed like this battle was lost, when it seemed like it had all been for naught, she saw hope on the hill above her. Justin stood on a ledge looking down at her, an expression of horror on his face.

Philomena experienced great relief at the sight of him. Somehow Justin would defeat the demon and rescue her. She had no idea how a mortal man could defeat an immortal spirit, but she felt confident that this man would somehow find a way.

Then a shocking idea occurred to her: perhaps Justin could not see the demon. She realized that, if the demon was invisible to Justin, she would appear to be an insane woman fighting against an imaginary enemy. If he already had doubts about her emotional stability, this would confirm his doubts about her as a suitable partner. He might turn and walk away. All these fears flashed through her mind in an instant.

However, he did not turn away. With a shout of

defiance, Justin jumped off the ledge. As he fell toward Philomena and the demon, a gleaming sword appeared in Justin's right hand.

Hearing the shout, the demon looked up and started to call forth power to hurl at Justin, but there was not enough time. Justin landed directly on the demon, his feet slamming into the demon's stomach. Justin drove the sword downward through the demon's chest, skewering his enemy to the ground.

The demon bellowed hideously before going silent and evaporating into nothingness. Even its black robes shriveled up and disappeared.

Justin's reassuring hands rested on Philomena's shoulders.

"Darling, open your eyes," he said.

"My eyes?" she asked dreamily.

"Yes. The demon is gone. I cast him out. I have been praying over you for the last hour."

She opened her eyes and found herself still in bed. It took her a few seconds to become oriented to her surroundings.

"Justin, you got here in time." She looked at him

lovingly. "The demon was trying to take possession of me."

"Well, he failed."

"How did you know that I was in danger?"

"The girls appeared to me in a dream and told me what was happening to you. I got over here as quickly as I could. In fact, the girls expedited my trip here by using their powers."

"Those girls are wonderful, and so are you." She leaned forward to hug Justin.

Although Philomena felt happy and relieved, she sensed that all was not yet right. The air seemed to tingle with energy.

Justin, too, perceived this. He hesitated mid-sentence. Something was happening -- something was coming. The house began to shake.

"Is it an earthquake?" Justin asked.

"No, it's some sort of power wave flowing through the house!" she exclaimed.

"You're right! And it's coming toward us!"

Just as he turned toward the door, two hellhounds burst through the open doorway and headed toward him.

Justin reached for his sword, but then remembered that he only had that weapon in the spiritual dimension. Here in the mortal world, he would have to fight empty-handed against the spectral beasts.

Time seemed to slow down as they leapt at him. From this close distance, the hellhounds looked completely otherworldly -- nightmare creatures come alive. They were lethal weapons wielded by a demonic intelligence.

Justin pulled back both his fists, planning to slam his fists into the hellhounds' snouts. Without a weapon, he knew that he had no chance of winning -- the beasts' razor-like teeth would tear him apart. However, he hoped that he could give Philomena time to flee from the room and escape.

Using all his strength, with his left and right fists, he hit both hellhounds simultaneously. That momentarily stopped them, but then they reared back in preparation for a strike at his throat.

To his astonishment, at that moment, Philomena jumped in front of him, placing her body between him and the hellhounds.

"Philomena, no! Get back! Run!" he shouted,

thinking that she was planning to sacrifice herself to save him.

However, Philomena had an arrow tightly clenched in both of her fists. With all her strength, Philomena slammed an arrow into each of the beasts. Their forward momentum caused the arrows to penetrate deeper than they would have otherwise.

Her left arrow went into the gaping maw of one beast and came out the back of its head. Her right arrow penetrated the forehead of the second spectral hound, digging deep into its skull.

The two hellhounds almost simultaneously exploded in a burst of energy that knocked both Justin and Philomena onto the floor. Momentarily dazed, they stared at the empty space where the hellhounds had been seconds earlier. The beasts were truly gone.

Justin took Philomena tenderly into his arms. "I came here to rescue you, but it turned out that you rescued me."

"You rescued me first; otherwise, I wouldn't have been able to help you," she said graciously.

Justin glanced at the two arrows, which now lay on

the floor.

"How did you happen to have those arrows at hand?"

"My father used to go bow hunting and these arrows belonged to him. Last week I cleaned out a closet in which some of my father's stuff was stored. When I opened the closet door, a quiver of arrows fell over and two of the arrows slid out onto the floor in front of me. As soon as I saw them, I recalled the importance of arrows in the story of Saint Philomena. I found it comforting to hold the arrows. Then I got the notion to show the arrows to my parish priest, so I brought them with me to Sunday morning Mass. He was not familiar with the details of the life of Saint Philomena, so he was happy to hear her story. He blessed the arrows for me."

"The arrows were blessed … they were anointed," Justin said reflectively. "That was why they were effective in destroying the hellhounds."

"Wow! Yes, that was why that worked!" she declared.

"Everything that happens in our lives neatly fits together like a jigsaw puzzle of vast complexity," Justin said. "If even a single piece is missing, the puzzle would be incomplete."

Philomena nodded. "Each piece of the puzzle fits into its proper place -- according to God's providential will."

"Thy will be done on the earth as it is in Heaven," Justin quoted from the prayer.

Philomena noticed that his right hand was bleeding. "You're injured, Justin!"

"Oh, I'm okay," he assured her. "The claws of one of the hellhounds made contact with me just a fraction of a second before you destroyed them."

"Let's rinse that cut out and bandage it," Philomena said, leading him toward the bathroom.

"All right," Justin agreed, turning himself over to her care.

In the springtime, their wedding was held at Our Lady of Victory Church. Somehow the location seemed appropriate.

Everyone in the congregation noticed the beauty of the two cherubic flower girls. The bride's guests assumed that the two girls were from the groom's family, while the groom's guests assumed that the girls were from the bride's family.

In actuality, the girls were from neither family, nor from the mortal world. Their identities were known only to Philomena and Justin.

By the time that the reception began, the two girls had disappeared. Some guests wondered briefly about their absence, but soon the girls were forgotten as the bride and groom and everyone around them were caught up in the joy of the day.

Joseph Rogers has other writings that include:
Realm of Haden: A Space-Age Fantasy
Maiden of Orleans: A Bayou Thriller
Sentinels at the Gates: A Telepathic Thriller
The Snow Maiden: A Suspense Thriller
Moonlight Warriors: A Tale of Two Hit Men
The Powers Unseen: A Supernatural Thriller
Travelers of Time
The Chronicles of Caroline Casey

Plays:
Child of Wonder: a modern Christmas drama
Tobias, a Traveler: a drama in two acts
Garden Sanctuary
My Friend's Obsession
The Sword of St. Louis: a romantic drama
Who Said It? : a whodunnit in two acts

Stories in Verse:
A Magical, Mystical Christmas Mystery
Essential Things
Wally the Wacky Wizard
Sprite of the Light: A Fairy Tale
A Princess and her Five Suitors: A Fairy Tale
The Mysterious Gift

The author's website is ***JoeRogers.homestead.com***

Made in the USA
Monee, IL
20 October 2023